At the Dentist

Design and Art Direction

Lindaanne Donohoe Design

Illustrations

Penny Dann

Picture Credits

© Barbara Filet/Tony Stone Images: cover
© Gregg Andersen/Gallery 19: 6, 8
© Jack McConnell: 12, 14, 16, 17, 18, 22, 24, 28
© Laura Elliot/Comstock, Inc.: 3, 10
© Margaret Miller, Science Source/Photo Researchers: 30
© Peter Pearson/Tony Stone Worldwide: 4
© Robert E. Daemmrich/Tony Stone Worldwide: 20
© Zigy Kaluzny/Tony Stone Images: 26

Library of Congress Cataloging-in-Publication Data

Greene, Carol.

At the dentist / by Carol Greene.
p.   cm.
Summary: Simple text and photographs describe
a visit to a dentist's office and what happens
there during a typical day.
ISBN 1-56766-468-7 (alk. paper)
1. Dentistry—Juvenile literature. 2. Dentists—Juvenile literature.
[1. Dentistry. 2. Dentists.]   I. Title.

RK63..G733   1998   97-31354
617.6—dc21   CIP
                                                AC

At the Dentist

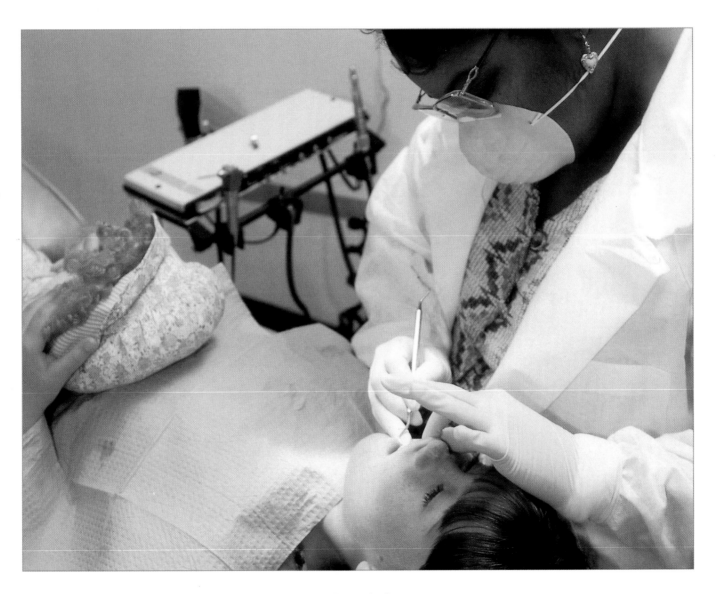

By Carol Greene

The Child's World®, Inc.

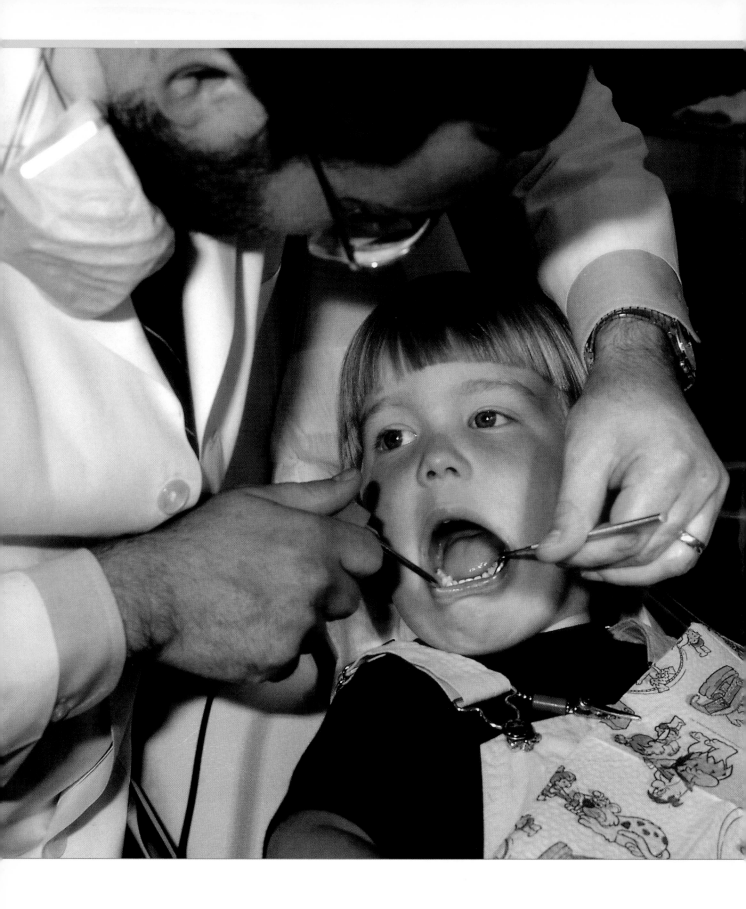

Three dentists work in this office.

One dentist works just with children.

One dentist works just with adults.

One dentist helps make crooked teeth straight.

He works with both children and adults.

The dentist that makes crooked teeth straight is called an orthodontist. Can you say this word?

LA-DA-DA-DA-DEE!

Soft music plays in the waiting room.

There are books for children and magazines.

Sometimes there are even puzzles and games!

SNAP! CLICK!

This girl is playing with a puzzle while she waits.

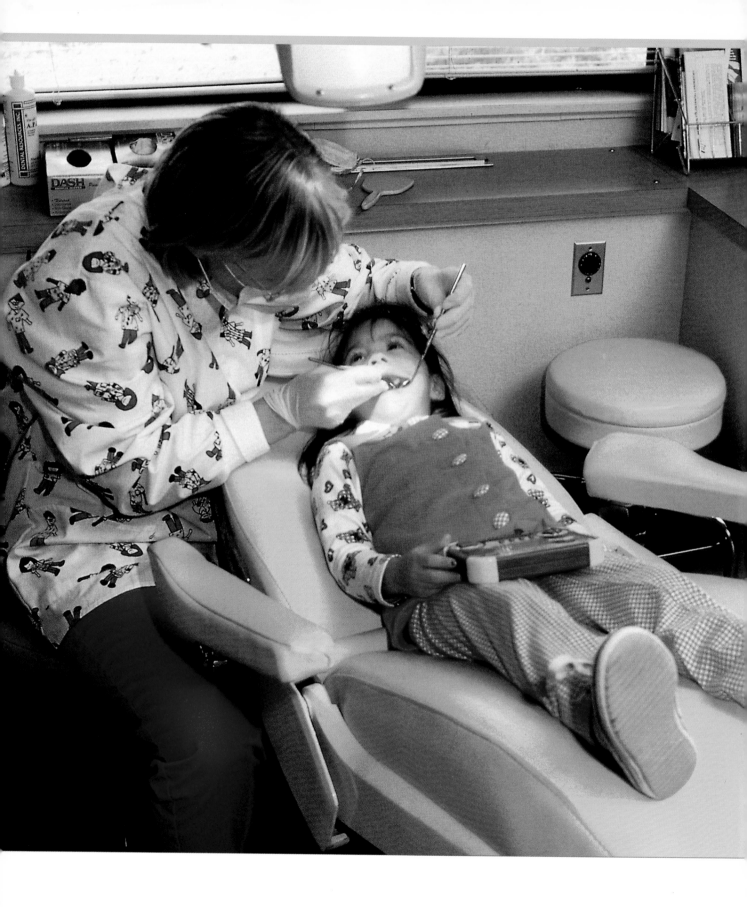

The children's dentist works here.

What a fancy chair!

HUMMM!

It goes up and down.

CLICK! CLICK!

It tips back and forth too.

The dentist fixes the chair so he or she can see into the patient's mouth.

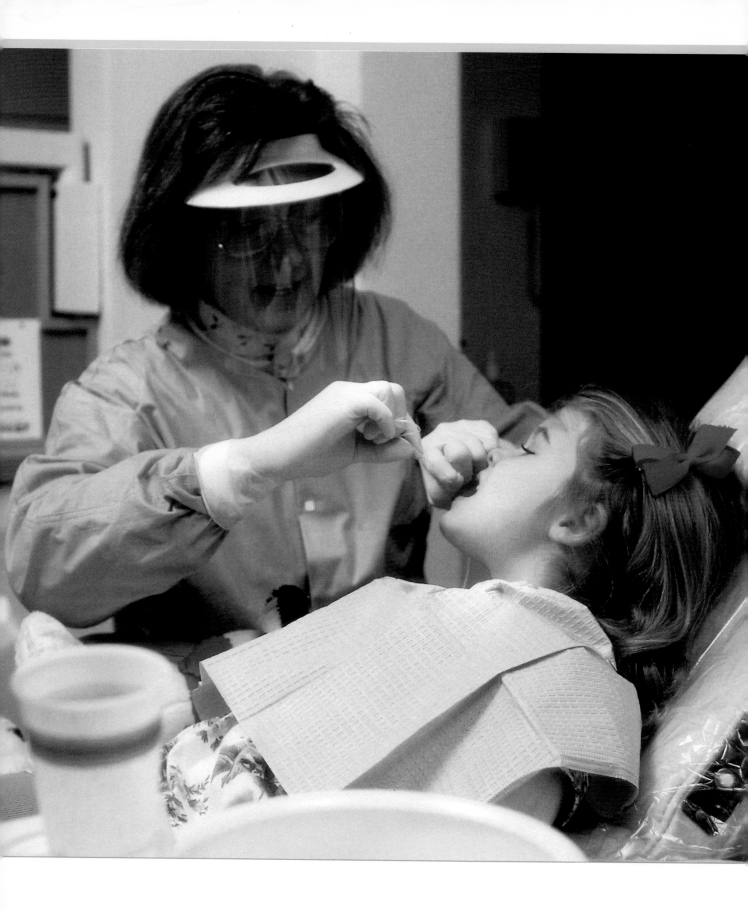

RUSTLE! RUSTLE!

People wear special clothes at the dentist's office.
Patients wear bibs to keep their clothes clean.
Dentists wear gloves and masks to protect the
patients from germs.

Can you see the dentist's special gloves?

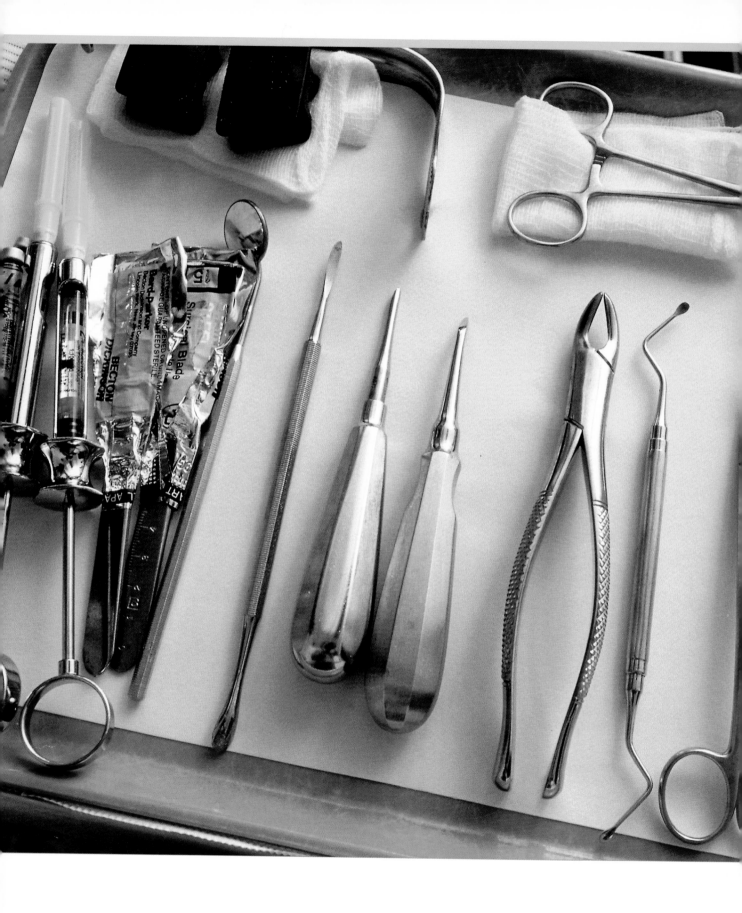

CLINK! CLANK!

Look at all these tools.

The dentist uses some tools to check teeth.

She uses others to clean teeth.

And she uses others to fix teeth.

A dental hygienist uses different tools to clean teeth.

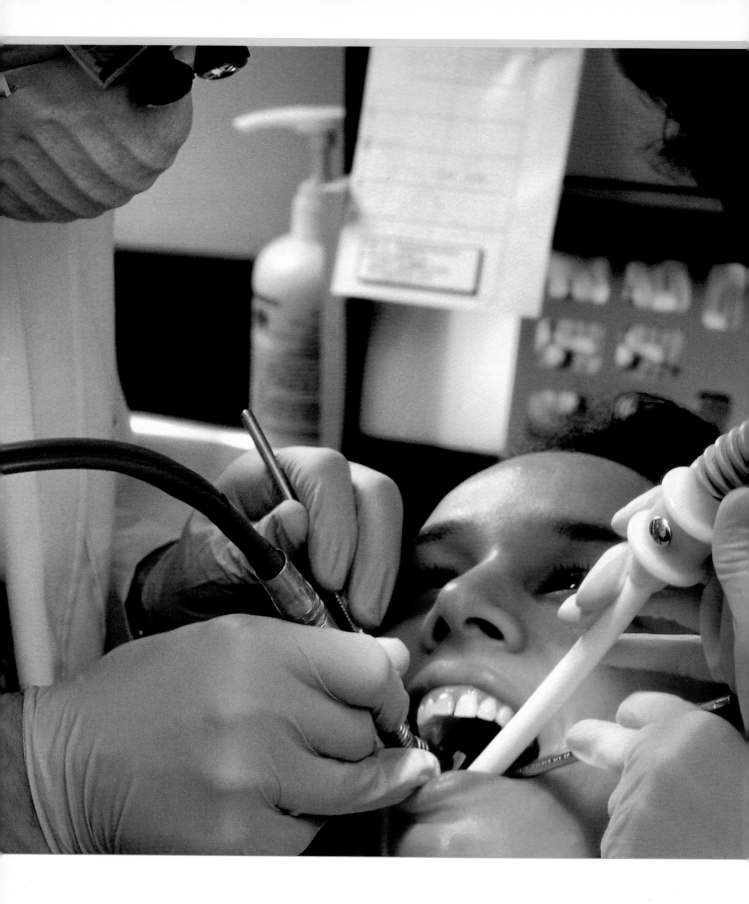

WHISSH!

This machine rinses teeth clean.
Another machine sucks water out
of the patient's mouth.
SLURP! SLURP!

Dentists need
to work
on dry teeth.

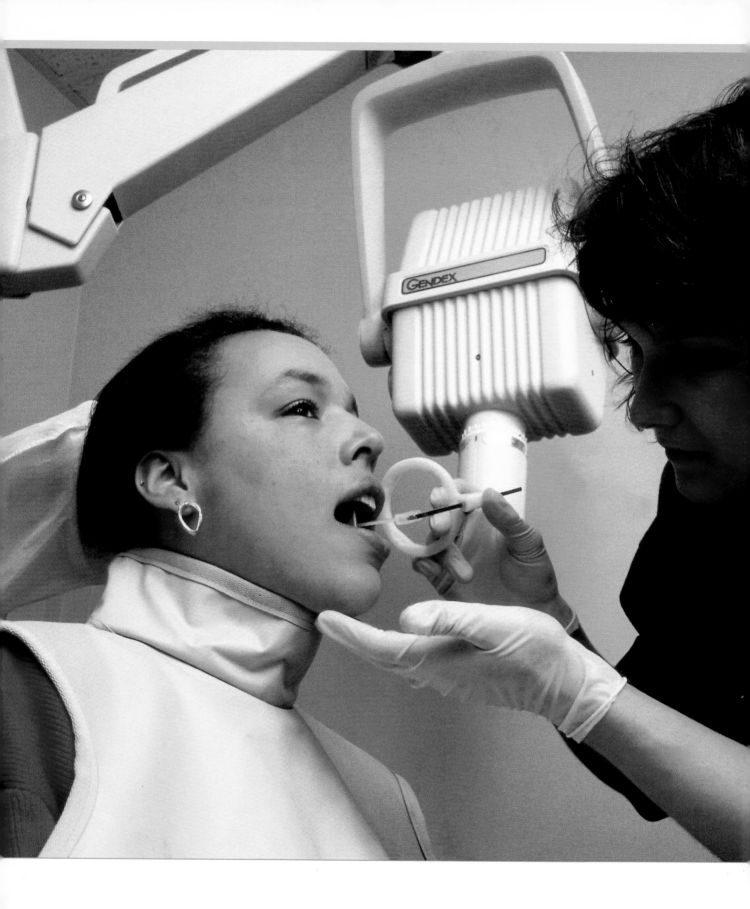

BZZT!

The X-ray machine takes pictures of teeth. The dentist develops the pictures here. Now she can see if the patient has any holes in her teeth. They are called cavities.

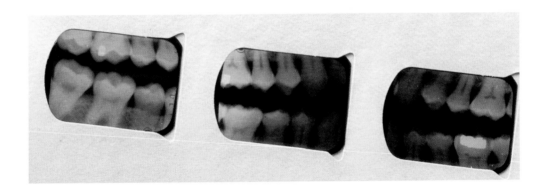

WOW! This patient has great teeth.

WHIRRR!

The dentist uses a high-speed drill

to clean out a tooth.

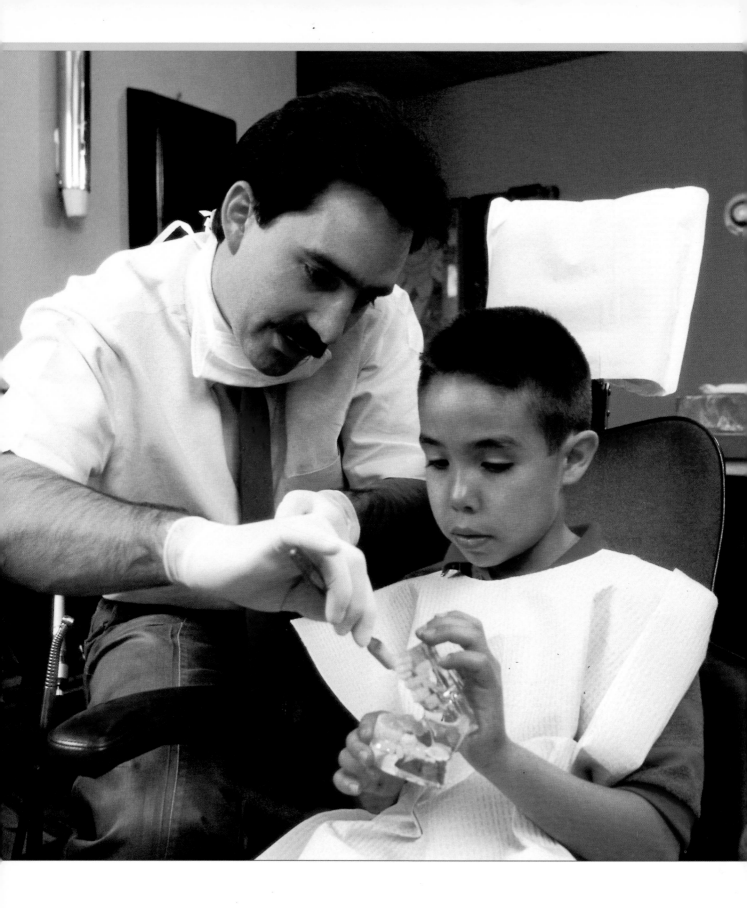

SWISH!

The dentist teaches this patient how to brush his teeth. Brushing helps keep teeth clean and healthy.

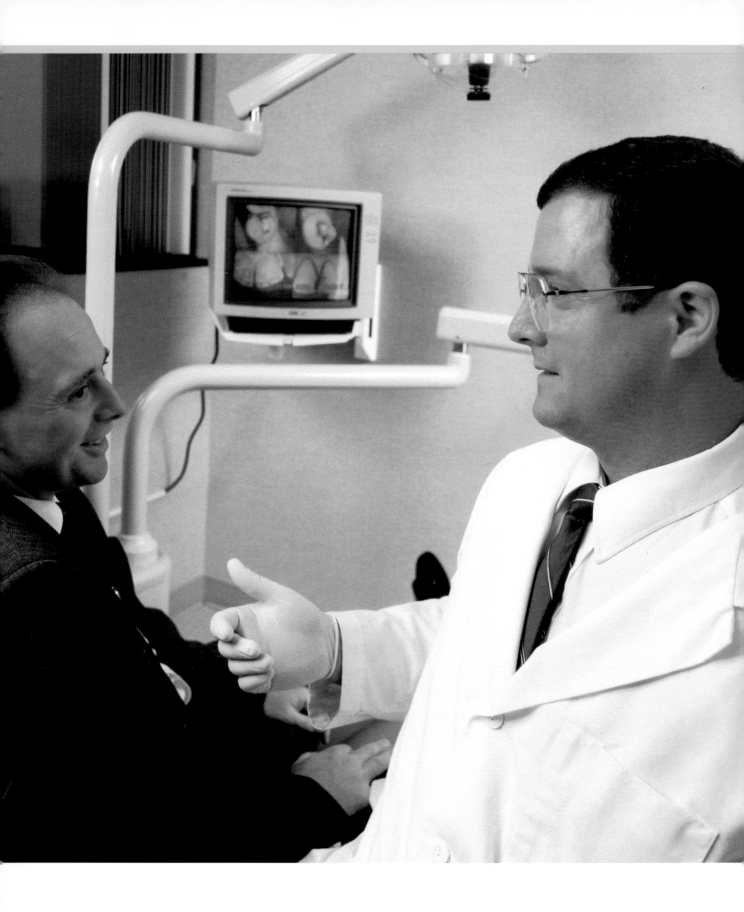

The dentist who works with adults does
many of the same jobs the children's dentist does.
But he does different things, too.
This patient needs false teeth.

False teeth are also called dentures.

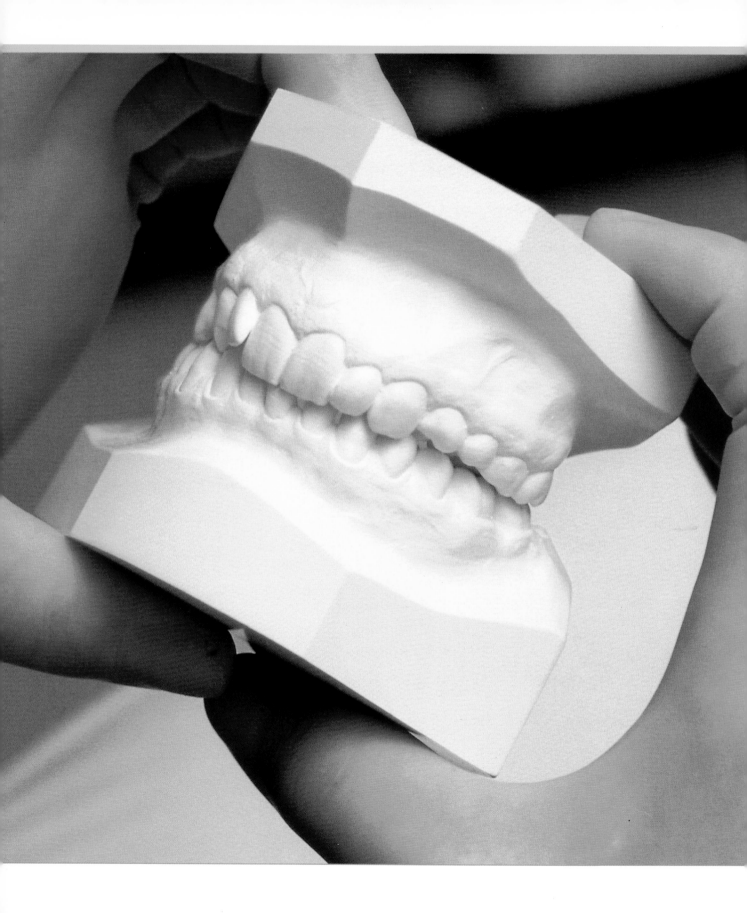

CHOMP!

The man bites into a soft pad.

Now the dentist can see the shape of his gums.

When the false teeth are made, the patient will be able to eat better. But false teeth are never as good as real teeth.

So take care of your teeth!

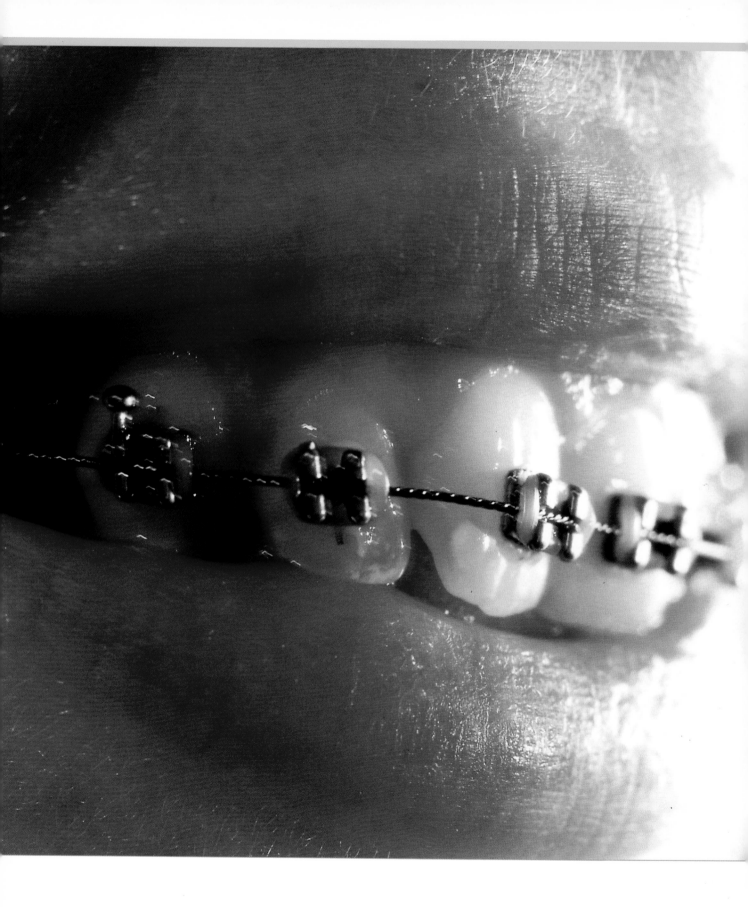

Sometimes people have crooked teeth.

This dentist can fix that. He is an orthodontist.

He puts braces on the crooked teeth.

The braces push the teeth very gently.

Both children and adults may need braces.

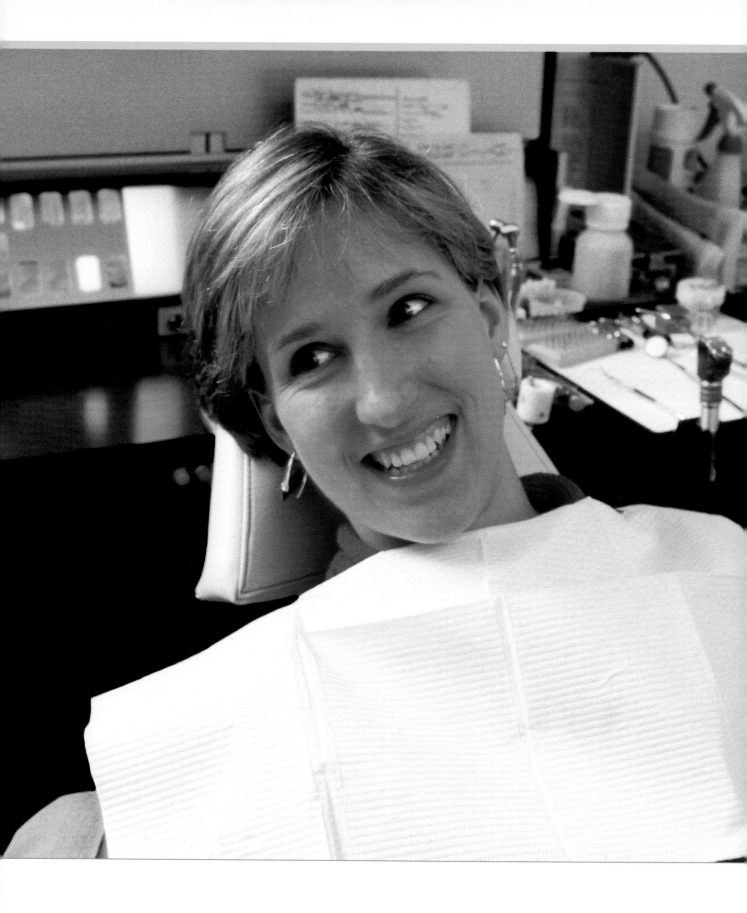

At last the teeth are straight.

Off come the braces!

Now the patient has a great smile.

Back to the children's dentist for a minute.

LOOK!

Good patients get to pick out a new toothbrush.

Dentists really do want their patients to be happy.

Glossary

braces — metal wires used to straighten teeth

cavities — holes in teeth where germs have gathered and caused damage

dental hygienist — a person trained to clean teeth

dentures — a set of false teeth

drill — a machine built to make holes

germs — things too small to be seen. Germs carry disease.

orthodontist — a dentist who is trained to straighten and adjust teeth

patient — a person getting medical treatment

X-ray machine — a device that takes pictures of the inside of things;
for example, an X-ray photograph through your skin will show bones

About the Author

Carol Greene has written over 200 books for children. She also likes to read books, make teddy bears, work in her garden, and sing. Ms. Greene lives in Webster Groves, Missouri.